Dating Mixtapes
Greatest Hits & Heartbreaks

Tracy-Ann D. Thorpe

Dating Mixtapes Greatest Hits & Heartbreaks

Published by Good Jinx, Inc.

©2025 by Tracy-Ann D. Thorpe.

All rights reserved. Printed in the United States of America. Published online by Good Jinx, Inc. Cover design and interior layout by Tracy-Ann D. Thorpe.

Print ISBN: 979-8-9992410-0-9

The publisher prohibits reproduction, distribution, or transmission of any part of this publication by any means, including photocopying, recording, or other electronic or mechanical methods, without prior written permission, except for brief quotations used in reviews, educational analyses, or scholarly work.

This is a work of fiction. While drawing inspiration from personal experiences and emotional truths, I fictionalized the characters and events for dramatic purposes. Any resemblance to actual persons, living or dead, is purely coincidental.

For inquiries or permissions, please contact:

Email: info@goodjinx.com

Website: www.goodjinx.com

First Edition

Dedicated to the ones who've loved and lost.
And to the ones still brave enough to love again.
May this book be your refuge.

Contents

The Playlist

1. Dec 11th

2. Make You Mine

3. All To Me

4. Garden Kisses

5. World We Created

6. Are you even real - (Teddy Swim's)

7. July 16th

8. Tryna Be

9. Last Heartbreak Song (Ayra Starr)

10. Lie Again

11. Vanish

12. Still Your Best

13. Fields

14. Let Me Go

15. Take Time (Interlude)

16. For Tonight

17. Like I Want You

18. Lost Me

19. When It's All Said And Done

20. Favorite Mistake

21. Stuck On You

22. Heartbreak Anniversary

23. Scarred

24. Unholy Matrimony

25. At Least we Tried

Set the Mood

Pick your vibe. Play the songs, read the story. Or read the story, then play the song. Your choice. This isn't just a book. It's a mixtape.

Disclaimer:

This playlist is a creative companion to the book Dating Mixtapes: Greatest Hits & Heartbreaks. It was curated to reflect the emotional themes and narrative arc of the story. I am not affiliated with, endorsed by, or in partnership with GIVĒON or any other artists featured on this playlist. All rights to the music, lyrics, and recordings are the property of their respective copyright holders. This playlist is provided solely for inspirational and storytelling purposes.

The First Encounter
Track 1

Inspired by: Dec 11th

Q & A

Q: Do you remember the exact moment when your life changed without warning?

A: Man, yes, and I remember how it felt like yesterday. That time in my life changed me, and I can't tell you if it's for better or worse.

1

At 6pm on a rainy Tuesday, Chris felt a void, unsure of what it was. He melted into his couch for 2 days after learning that the company hadn't chosen him for the project. When he finally got up, it was to look for food. Making multiple trips back and forth to the kitchen, trying to decide what he was in the mood for. It wasn't his hunger he was trying to feed. It was a void. That uncomfortable feeling of being. Chris didn't want to think about anything, so feeding the void with food was the next best thing.

"Fuck!" He yelled on the last trip to the kitchen. Putting his jacket on, and slipped his foot into his slides. The door opened. Chris tossed his hoodie over his head as he carelessly took two steps at a time from the 5th floor down. He crossed the street and entered the bodega, where he greeted the bodega cat, Oreo. Chris walked to the fridge and grabbed a pineapple soda, two honey buns, and a large bag of hot chips. As he walked toward the counter, he saw her. She stood with her skin shining from being covered in raindrops. He watched as a drop rolled off her cocoa-butter skin. As he walked past her, the smell of vanilla filled his nose. He put the snack on the counter, and he continued to watch her. Hair braided back and flipped over her shoulders. Her lips filled like a perfect cherry, her eyes bright. His eyes continued to trace her silhouette against the background and stopped at her feet.

"Jordans". She had on retro Jordans. Then she spoke. Her voice sounded like a New York siren:

"Take off some onions, please. Thanks."

That's when she turned and saw him staring.

She smiled as he fumbled to get his stuff on the counter after Ak tried to get his attention to finish the transaction. Once finished, he grabbed his bag and ran back to his apartment. The rain came down like bullets, shooting from the sky. At the door, Chris kicked off his slides, and then off came his rain-soaked jacket, which found its way to the floor and his comfort food on the counter.

What the fuck?

Why didn't you say something, you idiot?

She was standing right there.

Chris paced back and forth, thinking of what to do next. That's when he saw his computer desk. A bright yellow sticky note called to him.

You know what? I am gonna write to her.

Like, what's the worst that could happen?

She ignores me.

She gets me kicked out because she thinks I am a stalker.

Or we live together happily ever after.

Chris then goes to grab his decision-making tool; the coin his mother gave him. That once belonged to his father.

Heads I write it, tails I don't.

Let the universe decide my next move. Chris flipped the coin, and he watched it spin way longer than normal. Then it landed.

Heads.

"Looks like I am writing a note."

<u>Note</u>

To: 1A

Hey, I saw you at the bodega today. I hope they didn't put too much onions on your sandwich.

Because if they did, I would have to come back down and make them fix it.

From: 5D

Message me on IG if you get this @chris_the_hand-some_developer.

Without hesitation, Chris grabbed the note and ran carelessly down 5 flights of steps, placing the note on her door. He ran back up the steps, out of breath, afraid she would catch him in the act. Flopping onto his couch, he found refuge as his body attempted to calm his breathing. His gaze drifted to the snack on the counter. He no longer felt like it was gonna help because he was now hungry for something else. Unsure if she would message him. He sat daydreaming of what he would say to her. Time seemed to stand still as he walked to his window to see if he could glimpse her when she returned to the building. But nothing.

This went on, and he became uneasy, and that's when...

Ping!

<u>New Message</u>

@Jazz_way_2nice4u→@chris_the_handsome_developer

4

" Jasmine: Hey 5D Chris, why didn't you say something lol."

"It's her, fuck! What should I say?"

"Chris: Hey 1A, didn't want to get involved with a woman and her sandwich. I know that's serious business, lol."

"Jasmine: 5D, you ain't never lie. My name is Jasmine, so you can stop calling me 1A. And I assume your name is Chris."

"Chris: Your assumption is correct, Jasmine, and finally, it's nice to meet you."

"Jasmine: Likewise. I was wondering when you would talk to me."

"Chris: Wait, you wanted me to talk to you? Let me find out. If I had known that, I would have talked to you months ago".

"Jasmine: Better late than never."

"Chris: You're right. What are you doing tomorrow?"

Coffee
Track 2

Inspired by: Make You Mine

Q & A

Q: When did you first realize this wasn't just a crush, that you actually wanted to be with her?

A: Funny story, it was actually our first date. Something about her that made me want more. More of myself, more to give to her, just more. Her existence gave me purpose.

2

Chris instantly regretted his text. At first, his confidence was at a peak. He felt accomplished and unstoppable. However, he became humbled during the night watching as the hours changed. Lying awake, alert to every notification, hoping it was her messaging him back. By 3 a.m. he was completely restless and his mind would not let him sleep. Thoughts of her swarmed his mind until he did something.

Why would you write that?

She probably gets that a lot.

Nobody wants to hear that shit.

I look like a fool.

I can't text her now.

What if she just fell asleep?

Stressed out, Chris scrolled on her IG, admiring her and being careful not to touch the like button. He saw how happy she was with her friends and how she and her brother seemed close, always together. He noticed that her father had passed away. In his mind, he expressed his condolences, because he too had lost his father. For a moment, the memory of his father laughing played in his mind. It was unfortunate that the thing they had in common was death. To lose a parent is hard; he wouldn't wish it on his worst enemy. His scrolling continued, and that's when he found his way in.

Coffee!

He noticed how she would post about her coffee habits and how much she tried to quit, but never was strong enough to walk away from the liquid crack. Chris grabbed his sticky notes and his pen once more.

Note

To: 1A

Coffee or ice cream at 12 p.m.

() Yes

()No

From: 5D

PS, put this back on my door, and it's a date.

Unlike the first note, he observed this one to ensure its perfection. And that it was sending the right message. He wanted her to see that he was taking action. And not just asking her what she was doing, but he actually took action. This time he walked to the elevator, leaving his door open. His slouching shoulders, yawn and sudden lack of energy told him what he had been waiting for all night.

Chris woke up in the morning, barely opening his eyes. He grabbed his phone and saw the time. 11:30 a.m. Before another second could pass, he opened his phone to see if she had messaged him. But nothing, just a bunch of missed calls from scam likely numbers, spam texts, and his friend group chat with 120 messages. But no Jasmine.

He remembered his note, jumped out of bed, knocked over his reading lamp, rushed to the door and swung it open only to see nothing but a UPS delivery notice. He grabbed it.

Just as he was about to close the door, he saw the note on the floor. The blank side faced him. Unaware of what was on the other side, he rushed to pick it up. Chris turned the note over and saw that Jasmine had marked up his note with her own notes.

<u>Note</u>

To : 5D

<u>Coffee</u> or ice cream at ~~12 p.m.~~ 2 p.m.

(x) Yes

()No

From: 1A

PS, put this back on my door, and it is a date.

(It better be!)

XOXO

As Chris read the note, he got excited.

"Ok!"

"Ok!"

"Not bad, I got some time."Chris grabbed his phone and messaged her on IG.

<u>New Message</u>

@chris_the_handsome_developer →@Jazz_way_2nice4u

Chris: I got your note. Thank you for getting back to me. I'll see you later at 2 p.m. at the coffee shop up the block. Here's my number: 555-315-9090, text me.

The 3 little dots popped up and quickly disappeared.

<u>Text</u>

Jasmine: 555-769-4555 →Chris

555-769-4555: Hey I figured I got your number, so I might as well text you. I'll see you at 2. I may be a few minutes late, but I'll be there.

Chris: I am about to lock you in Jasmine with all the emojis.

He saved her name with heart emojis.

Jasmine : LOL.

Chris: LOL, see you later.

Letting out a deep breath, he set his alarm for 12:45 p.m., picked up his remote control for his system and played the game until his alarm went off. Not hurrying, he took his time: shit, shaved and showered. He got dressed and grabbed a banana. Took the elevator down. Chris walked up the block where he saw a teddy bear with sneakers on. His mind flashed back to the night he saw her. She had on the OG retro ones.

She got to be a sneaker-head. He walked into the store and examined all the teddy bears, looking for the one that matched her vibe. When he found one with a jersey and red sneakers. He bought it for her without hesitation. Unraveling his headphones, he walked into the coffee shop. An empty seat was by a window. Making his way over, he sat facing the street; He wanted to see her when she came. 25 minutes went by, and she still didn't come. Chris remind calm. He remembered she had told him she would be late.

Lost in his music, he felt a tap on his shoulder. Turning around, he saw it was her. He had a big smile on his face, and so did she as she reached up to give him a hug. Jasmine broke the silence.

"Hey, how are you?"

"I'm good, and you?"

"That's good. I'm cool, just got off work. Sorry, I'm late, by the way. Trains sometimes skip stops because of construction."

"It's cool, better to be late than never. You wanna go get some caffeine now or later?"

"Now please, I am literally a caffeine fiend."

"How many cups a day?"

"Sometimes 2, sometimes 3 on a long day. I really need to chill with the coffee."

As they walked to the counter, he turned and asked her what she was getting.

She responded.

"It's complicated". Jasmine gave Chris her order. Her mouth moved faster than he could catch on. Looking at her with confusion, he told her to order. God forbid he messed up; She might mess him up.

"That's a mouthful, Jazz."

"It's not that bad." She playfully pushed his shoulder. The barista asked for the order. Jasmine ordered. Chris watched her lips move in slow motion. Her tiny nose ring sparkled in the light. She turned and asked him what he wanted, and he responded.

" Whatever you've got."

She asked him whether he was allergic to anything. He shook his head no and handed her his credit card. She taped the card and handed it back to Chris. As she moved to pick up, Chris followed behind her. She navigated the coffee shop as if it were her home. Jasmine grabbed their drinks, handing one to Chris.

"Let me take you to my spot." Jasmine said as they walked up the steps of the coffee shop.

She pointed to a seat with a round window and a round table. Like a gentleman, he pulled out her seat and watched her as she sat gracefully. Chris broke the ice with the questions, looking at his large coffee cup.

"What exactly is this? "

"It's a caramel macchiato with extra caramel with an extra shot; you would like it."

Chris looked at his cup.

"You know what's crazy? This is my first time drinking coffee."

"Really like you never ever had it."

"Naw, let me not lie. Maybe once as a kid, but it was nasty, and I never tried it again."

"Okay! Look at me being your first. I love it."

"What do you mean?" Chris questioned.

"I am popping your coffee cherry, Chris, and it's gonna be good. You're gonna be a junkie like me soon." They both laughed. Chris took a sip and nodded his head in approval.

"See, I told you." She said.

"It's good, I like it." Chris said as he inspected the cup to see if it would give him the ingredients .

"So the other night you said that you wondered when I would talk to you. What did you mean by that?" He asked.

"Well, I saw you when you moved into the building, and I went outside just to get a better look, but I don't think you saw me. I saw you a few more times at the mailbox. You said nothing. I figured you didn't want me, so I cried every night."She made a sad face.

"I didn't mean to make you cry, boo."

"I was joking; I was not crying silly." She laughed.

"Oh! So you got game, I see."

"Not game-baby jokes." Sticking her tongue out ever so slightly, she made the cutest face. He smiled.

"I have been wanting to get to know you from the first day I saw you, but I didn't think you would like me, and I thought you had a man. So I had to be calm about my approach."

"I don't have a man. I'm kind of talking to someone; It was getting serious, but now it's just fizzling out. I am interested in getting to know someone else, though. Is that okay with you?" She took a sip of her coffee and flirted with her eyes.

"Diamonds don't crack under pressure. Not gonna lie, I don't see you talking to him much longer."

"Is that so?" She made a curious face. "So what's your relationship status, Mr. Confidence?"

"I was messing with someone for like a year. But when I started working on my project, she dipped out on me. Trust me, I am not mad about it, because I would not be here with you right now."

Jasmine smiled. The two continued talking for hours, not leaving the store until they noticed the barista stacking the chairs. They walked back to their building hand in hand. He walked her to the door, hugged her, and told her goodnight. He stayed at her door until he heard her door lock from the inside.

Chris jogged up the steps, opened his door and threw his body on the couch. His mind racing .

Shit! I did that.

"Lock in, she don't know, we locked in like white on rice. He joked to himself.

Chris pulled out his phone to send Jackson a voice note.

Voice Note

Chris →Jackson

"Chris : Bro, lock in, it's 10 p.m. I just got back. I never had this much to say to a girl. Shorty is everything. Man, if you don't hear from me, just know she got ya boy in his feelings. That's wifey."

"Jackson: Bro, you say that about everyone ,haha."

"Chris : Naw, this one is different."

"Jackson: I hear you, fam. Yo, make sure you re-submit your project, bro. They weren't ready for you before, but I think they understand now. That other project was a flop. Your shit is way better."

"Chris: I'll do it in the morning."

Chris wanted to text Jasmine, but he didn't know what to write. It was like they talked about everything, and he didn't want to force a conversation. Plus, he had already said good night. So he stuck to what's been working. He grabbed a sticky note and wrote.

Note

To: 1A

What was the name of that coffee drink again ?
From: 5D.

The Other Guy
Track 3

Inspired by: All To Me

Q & A

Q: Now that you know she was seeing someone else, what were some challenges?

A: Her seeing someone else wasn't a challenge. I knew we would be together... regardless. It just so happens that as soon as we started talking, that was it for him.

3

~◦~

Chris had just gotten off the train. The day was regular until it wasn't. Noise filled the hallway outside her apartment, not the kind he was used to. This wasn't laughter or music or neighbors being loud. This was something different. Shouting and aggression all coming from 1A. The deep voice that wasn't hers wailed into the hallway. Then a pause, then louder, some words muffled, others sharp and cut deep.

"You're a bitch!"

A voice coming from 1A shouted. Chris froze outside Jasmine's door. His first instinct was to knock. But his hand stalled halfway there. She wasn't his girl, not yet. And whatever was going on in there, it sounded like a lover's argument. Not in his lane. But something inside him, something protective, didn't want to just walk away either. Chris quickly reached his hand into his pocket searching for his phone. He grabbed it; His heart sank once he noticed it was lifeless. He moved fast, five flights up, two steps at a time. Back at his apartment, he plugged it in like his life depended on it and stared at the black screen until it lit up. As soon as the screen loaded, he typed.

Text

Chris →Jasmine

Chris: Are you okay? Do you need me to come down?

Her response came fast.

Jasmine: I'm fine. He's leaving.

Chris read it, then reread it. But he could not sit with it .

Chris: You sure?

Jasmine: Yeah. He's just upset. I told him I was done. He doesn't understand. He thinks I wasn't giving enough back. But I'm over it.

Chris leaned back on his couch. A weird mix of relief and something else. As questions ran through his mind. *If the guy did everything, why did she end it? Was it because of him? Was he the reason?* He shook it off. Twenty minutes later, she texted him.

Jasmine: You can come down now.

He didn't even hesitate. The elevator would take too long. Chris flew down the steps like his feet were on fire. He knocked once. Jasmine opened the door as if she'd been standing on the other side, waiting. Once inside, he noticed it right away. The teddy bear with the sneakers. The one he bought for her before their first date. Sitting on a shelf next to framed photos and scented candles, there it was. She hadn't hidden it. It was front and center. That meant something.

"You good?" he asked.

"Yeah. It's handled. Relax. I'm cool." She nodded.

"You sure?"

"I'm sure."

"Can I get a hug?" he asked. She didn't answer. Just stepped toward him. He wrapped his arms around her slowly, like he didn't want to press too hard or let go too soon. Her head fit perfectly under his chin. His arms became her shelter. He held her there, keeping her warm, while the rest of the world kept spinning somewhere outside the door.

"Thanks for coming," she whispered.

They sat down on her couch. The tension in the room was gone.

"Do you want anything to drink?" she asked.

"Nah, I'm good. I just wanted to check on you for real."

She looked away for a second. Then back at him.

"I told him I was done. We've been doing the whole not-serious thing for months. But I'm done with not being taken seriously. I want something real. I'm tired of being around where I don't feel wanted."

Chris said nothing at first. Just let it sit in the air with them.

"I'd rather be where I'm wanted," she said again, this time looking straight at him.

Their eyes held longer than usual. Something unspoken passed between them.

Chris leaned in slowly. No rush, just the moment. His hand grazed her cheek, asking a question without words. She answered without speaking. Her lips met his, soft and curious. The kiss was like a finger rubbing gently across rose petals, examining the velvet texture. The kiss that made time shift just a little. When they pulled back, Chris smiled.

"You taste like coffee." He joked. Jasmine raised an eyebrow.

"And you taste like trouble." She flirted back.

They both laughed.

Then he went back for more.

Close To You
Track 4

Inspired by: Garden Kisses

Q & A

Q: When did it stop being just flirting and turn into something real?

A: The night we stopped pretending we weren't falling for each other. We never actually said I love you, but I knew what it was .

4

The room was quiet, lit only by the low golden hue of a lamp she kept on the dresser. Soft enough to cast a warm hug, but just bright enough to see. Music played low from her speaker, the familiar sound of romance. The song you listen to until it becomes embedded in part of a memory. Chris sat at the edge of her bed, fingers tracing the rim of his water glass. Jasmine stood by the window, the city lights flickering against her silhouette like dancing stars.

He walked towards her, pressing his hands on the window frame. Neither of them spoke. It was in the way she turned toward him, deliberate, gentle, like she'd been rehearsing it in her head. She walked away barefoot, braids loose, her oversized T-shirt falling just above her hips. He followed her. Their closeness pulled the air out of the room.

Hearts beating loud enough to fill the silence. She placed her hands on his chest, where they rested before traveling elsewhere. Moving across his body, feeling every curve of his muscular figure. Like she was feeling the rhythm before joining the song. His fingers moved to her waist, brushing her skin where the shirt stopped.

"You good?" he asked.

"I'm sure," she whispered.

Then she kissed him slowly, like she was trying to memorize the shape of his mouth.

He kissed her back, but didn't rush her. Letting her lead the unspoken conversation with their tongues.

His lips found her cheek, her jaw, the curve of her neck. His hands found sacred places. He gave her kisses you don't give just anyone. Jasmine tilted her head back, eyes closed, breathing shallow. Her fingers found the back of his head. He stood up as she helped him pull the hoodie off. Then his shirt, leaving little to no clothing between them.

She backed up toward the bed, pulling him with her. Her legs touched the sheets first, but she didn't sit until she had no place to go. They eased into it seamlessly. More clothes came off the way petals fell from a flower, one by one. The light hit her shoulder as she leaned back, and Chris paused, just to look. Wanting to save this moment for the rest of his life.

"You're staring," she whispered.

"I know...I'm allowed." He kissed her collarbone. Her shoulder. The inside of her wrist. Not because he had to. He wanted her to know she was safe with him. He eased into her. Her body arched into his like they'd done this a thousand times in another life. She gasped, fingers digging into his skin. They moved together the way water moves, with curves. When it was over, they didn't speak. She laid her head on his chest. He played with her fingers, her hair and kissed her lips. They didn't talk about what came next. They didn't need to.

Don't Want To Leave
Track 5

Inspired by: World We Created

Q & A

Q: What's your favorite memory with Jasmine? When it felt like nothing outside the two of you existed?

A: I remember one day I stayed at her place and I didn't want to leave. It wasn't like the other times I stayed with other women. I wanted them to go. I wanted to go. But this time, I didn't want the day to end.

5

~◻~

The day started with a message. A simple vibration. Just enough to break the rhythm of the morning. Chris blinked against the light leaking through the curtains. He'd been up for hours but hadn't moved. Stuck somewhere between now and yesterday, thinking about Jasmine, about the way her eyes smiled without trying, how she folded into him when they watched movies, how nothing didn't even matter anymore. Everything outside them was noise. He finally reached for his phone.

Text

Erica →Chris

Erica: Can we talk?

Three words and one open door. Chris stared at it, watched it, hoping it vanished on its own. It didn't. Of course, it didn't. Erica never left. She just paused, waited, circled back like hurricane season. Predictable, yet always disorienting.

He tossed the phone onto the bed and sat up, elbows on knees, palms over his face. The room was quiet. Too quiet for his loud mind. Because here's the truth, Chris didn't know what the hell he wanted. There was comfort in Erica, familiarity. They had a history. She knew his angles, his old scars. She had him once. And now. She was back. And Jasmine was everything he didn't know he needed. Soft, funny, strong, wild with sweetness. But the feeling was still new, still being built, with no guarantees.

He didn't want to ruin what they had. But he also didn't want to lie to himself. Something in him was still unsure and open to Erica.

Chris grabbed his phone again. Not to answer her but to call Jackson. It rang once.

"Yoooo." Jackson's voice came through the speakers. Chris didn't waste time.

"Bro, Erica hit me up." A long pause. Jackson exhaled as if he'd been holding that breath for a while.

"Damn! What'd she say?"

"She said she wants to talk."

"Talk or talk?"

"You know the answer to that."

"Shit!"

"Yeah." Chris leaned back, staring at the ceiling like it held the answer. Jackson's voice broke the silence.

"Are you thinking about talking to her?" Chris didn't respond right away. That was the answer.

"I dunno, man. I'm with Jasmine now. Well, not official-official, but you know. It feels real. But Erica is Erica."

"Yeah," Jackson said, thoughtful. "But Jasmine's now. Erica's the past. Are you trying to decide between a past life and the life you have now, the one that's just getting good?" Chris let that sit. "Look, I ain't telling you what to do," Jackson continued. "But all I'm gonna say is, stick with what makes you happy. Not what's easy. Not what's familiar. Happy!"

Chris closed his eyes. Jasmine's laugh came to him. The way she played with the straw in her iced coffee. Her bare feet, toes making shapes on the carpet when she forgot her slippers. The way she always remembered to ask about his project's even when he didn't believe in them anymore.

"Yeah," he said. " You're right."

"I know," Jackson said. "Fuck Erica, bro". Smirking through the phone. Chris hung up, pulled on his sweats, and texted Jasmine.

Text

Chris →Jasmine

Chris: Are you busy? I wanna see you.

The response came two minutes later.

Jasmine: I'm home. Come down.

When Jasmine opened the door, she was barefoot. Hair tied up. No makeup. Tank top and shorts, effortless.

"Hey stranger," she said, stepping aside. Chris smiled, but said nothing, just hugged her.

"You good?" she asked. "You just randomly messaged me. I haven't heard from you all day."He shook his head, brushed it off.

"Yeah. I was just in my head this morning; I needed to clear it. That project is kicking my ass."

She looked at him for a second longer, as if she could read the pause in his voice, but she didn't press. Chris thought about telling her about the text from Erica, but couldn't bring himself to do it.

"I made dinner. Are you hungry?" She asked.He nodded and said.

"Hell yeah." He played around pretending to lick his fingers. They ate together on her couch, the TV low, their legs touching. Jasmine told a story about a customer at work who tried to return shoes after wearing them. She liked her job but considered stepping down. Being a general manager took too much time away from photography. The way she told him stories, he would listen just to hear her speak. He laughed and let her voice carry him away into bliss.

Later, after rinsing the dishes and dimming the lights, they sat. No rush to go home. Her head rested on his shoulder. His fingers played with hers. Chris didn't know if the world would ever slow down enough for him to figure everything out. In that moment, with her body pressed against his and the smell of cocoa butter and vanilla on her skin, he knew peace. He felt no compulsion to run, fix, or choose. He felt at ease. This was where he knew he belonged. Not in the future, not in the past. But right here. Was where he needed to be.

Love, Actually
Track 6

Inspired by: Are You Even Real?

Q & A

Q: So, did it ever feel too perfect, like maybe the feelings were too good to last?

A: Nah, I actually had the opposite feeling. I felt like it was too good, and I wanted it to last. I felt like it had to last. There was no reason for it not to be. She was the first person I would call. Not Jackson, not my mom. Jasmine was it. That's when I knew she was the one.

6

~🖭~

Chris had barely finished his breakfast when the meeting invite dropped.

<u>Invite</u>

Team Sync: 8:30 a.m. mandatory.

He was already deep in code, debugging a function for the landing page redesign. He clicked the invite, heart tight in his chest. For weeks, he'd been chasing this. His contract was almost up for renewal, and the project he pitched had been in limbo. The last time he got passed over, he stayed home for two days and ate nothing but honey buns and hot chips. He wasn't doing that again.

He walked into the conference room with a tight jaw and a calm demeanor. The director, the manager and two other senior developers were already in their seats. What happened next blurred slightly. The words: "We're moving forward with your proposal. Congratulations Chris, you're full-time!" said his manager. He heard claps, a few jokes. He nodded and thanked them. His mind was racing, but his body stayed still. Shaking hands and saying thank you again and again. Once the celebration was over, he went back to his desk. Unlocked his phone, hovered over Jackson's name and stopped.

He stared at the screen, then quickly tapped Jasmine's name. It rang once, twice. Then her voice.

"Hey baby!" she said, breathless and warm, like she'd been rushing to answer.

Chris smiled for the first time all morning.

"Are you busy?"

"No, what's up?"

"I got it." There was a pause.

"Got what?"

"The job, full-time, my project got approved. I'm in." The silence on the line broke with a squeal that made his headphones buzz.

" OMG! Chris! Shut up! Are you serious?"

"I'm deadass. They told me at the meeting."

"I'm so proud of you," she said, and the way her voice landed in his ear made something in his chest swell. "You deserve this. You really, really do." He exhaled and looked down at his hands.

"You were the first person I called. I didn't even call my mom."

"You sure you wanna admit that out loud?" she teased.

"Yeah, I do." She was quiet for a second.

"Come over as soon as you get off. I want to celebrate with you." He nodded, still smiling.

"Say less."

Chris left work early. He told his boss he had plans, and for once, they said. "Go! Celebrate."

By 4 p.m., he was on the block, sneakers barely hitting the pavement before he knew it. His hands reached to open the door of her apartment.

"SURPRISE!"

The room burst, Jackson, Bianca, Marcus and even his cousin Darnell. They popped bottles, balloons floated to the ceiling, and music pulsed. from a corner speaker.

Jasmine stood in the center of it all. Hair down, lip gloss shining, arms open. She walked up to him. Without saying a word, and pulled him into a kiss. So deep he barely remembered anyone else was in the room. For a moment, the world shrank. His eyes stayed closed longer than necessary, and when they opened, it was like light had changed his location from heaven to earth. Everyone danced, laughed and enjoyed themselves. Chris did not miss a moment to hug everyone. But he centered his mind on Jasmine the whole time; she was his anchor. She refilled his drink before he asked. Checked in with him with just a look. She knew when to let him vibe and when to pull him into a moment.

And then it hit him. Around 6:30 p.m., after the third toast and a thousand "you did it." Chris stepped away. He needed a second. He walked into her room, closed the door behind him, and sat on the edge of her bed. The smell of her vanilla oil was everywhere. He looked down at his hands again. *How could something feel so perfect and still be real?* The door cracked.

"You good?" Jasmine asked, peeking in. He stood and gently closed the door behind her, locking it.

"Sit," he said, motioning her to the bed. She did quietly watching him. He stood in front of her, heart in his throat.

"I love you Jazz."

"Chris." She said as she tried to blink back her emotions.

" Dont say anything. I just... I need to say this. I love you. Not just saying it. Not like 'I love how you smell' or 'I love how you kiss.' I love you like… I never wanna lose you. You're the first person I wanna tell good news to. Whatever this is, it's the best thing that's ever happened to me. This runs deep for me."

"I love you too, Chris." She looked up at him, eyes full.

He exhaled, relief and awe washing over him like rain from the first night they spoke. He leaned in, and this time, the kiss was quieter, no cheers, no music, no crowd, eyes closed and back in heaven. Just her, him, the room, and a future that felt terrifyingly beautiful.

Chaos
Track 7

Inspired by: July 16th

Q & A

Q: So you weren't afraid to go all in?

A: I wasn't afraid, but when my ex Erica resurfaced, she brought chaos with her.

7

It had been six months. Half a year since the bodega. Since the sticky notes. Ever since his first sip of coffee, love has rewired his taste buds. Now he was here, button-down shirt tucked in, Jasmine's lip gloss sticky on his cheek. He sat next to her at the rehearsal dinner for her cousin. A candlelit banquet hall, one of those Brooklyn spots that could double as a club or a wine bar depending on the night, held them. Everyone looked nice. Couples looked in love. The groom-to-be stood at the front of the room, holding a champagne flute, trying to hold back tears.

"She's my peace. My partner. My home. She reminds me that love is worth the wait and worth the work."

Chris looked at Jasmine. She smiled. He didn't say it, but he felt it. Feelings ever so real that it could be them one day. He caught himself fantasizing about rings, sticky notes turned into vows. Mail with her name coming to his place, and little echoes of laughter coming from his apartment.

"Are you ready to go?" she whispered after dessert. He nodded yes and asked her if she was still going to hang out with her cousin. She answered yes; she had plans for a girls' night out; wine, music and probably dancing.

"Go have fun," he said, kissing her cheek. "Text me when you get back."

"Love you." She kissed him back.

"Love you, too."

By 9:07 p.m., Chris was home chilling in his gray sweat-pants, TV remote in one hand, phone in the other. Music from his speakers bounced off the walls. He scrolled aimlessly, not really watching the movie he settled on. He was just...floating. Thinking about the speech. He thought about Jasmine's hand in his as they exchanged vows one day, and how proud she always looked when people spoke of him. Then, his phone lit up. *Erica.* He stared at the name, throat tight. She had called a couple of weeks ago. He ignored it, telling himself he was past it.

But tonight, he picked up.

"Chris," she said, as if she had never stopped speaking his name.

His body tensed. Her voice still sounded like something familiar. Like a wrong turn, he used to go home. They talked, even though it felt wrong. Nothing deep at first. Just catching up, light laughs. That dangerous comfort plagued him. Then she asked.

"Can I come over?" He hesitated. Jasmine wouldn't be home until late. And this was just... talking, right? He thought about how she ended things with him for someone else; A part of him wanted closure.

"Yeah," he mumbled, unsure and biting down on his lip.

By 10:33 p.m., Erica was on his couch. Shoes off, hoodie laid out on the floor. The same perfume he had bought her now lingered in his apartment again. Chris tried to stay in control. But the lines blurred.

Their laughter got closer. The way she looked at him. She knew she still had keys to parts of him Jasmine hadn't unlocked yet. The things he was too ashamed to talk about or ask for. His primal urges came alive around Erica. She allowed him to bend her to his will. All the while he treated Jasmine like a flower. Then it happened; A touch on his thigh, a gentle touch of lips, a pause and another kiss. Before he could stop himself, his hands wrapped around her neck. Her hand on his, not to stop him, but to signal if he squeezed too hard.

The room felt small, hot, and the silence was loud. You could hear the clock ticking on the wall. *Tick Tock ,Tick Tock.* It echoed louder than the animalistic grunting that came from his sweaty frame. By the time it was over, Chris sat on the edge of the bed and stared at the floor. Erica was almost asleep. But Jasmine's voice popped in his mind, her voice in his head. *I love you.* He whispered back into the silence. *I'm sorry.* And it didn't make it better. Not even a little. Chris sat there, still shirtless, feet planted on the floor like the ground might move beneath him if he moved too fast. Erica breathed softly behind him, tangled in sheets she didn't belong in. His phone buzzed on the nightstand.

Text

Jasmine→ Chris

Jasmine: I'm heading back now, you up?

Chris didn't answer her text; He couldn't. He turned his phone face-down and stood. His legs felt heavy, like his body knew what his heart had been trying to tell him. He walked over to the bathroom.

Flicked on the light, and looked in the mirror, cleaning himself off. He hated what looked back. The guilt he felt contaminated him. He had stained something pure with his disloyalty. He walked back to the room and disrupted the peace that Erica had, telling her she needed to leave because he had work in the morning. Erica reached for her clothes, casually pulling her hoodie over her head like nothing had happened.

"Thanks for letting me come over," she said, voice soft, like they'd shared something romantic. Chris didn't respond.

At 11:58 p.m., he walked her out of the apartment. Each step felt like penance. His hand hovered near her back but never touched, almost like he was guiding her to exit. They reached the door first. She turned, expecting a kiss. He kissed her quickly with regret and offered her a nod.

"Goodnight," she said, slightly confused.

"Yeah. Night." He replied.

She walked into the dark and into her cab. Chris didn't go back up immediately. He stood in the hallway like a man who needed to bury a secret too heavy to carry upstairs. When he finally climbed the steps, it was like the air in his apartment had shifted.

The room felt small and uncomfortable. He dropped onto the couch and stared at the ceiling, chest hollowed out. He whispered to no one.

What the fuck did I just do?

And then, he heard the doorknob jiggle. Soft knock.

"Shit, Jasmine." He froze. Not because he was afraid she'd find out, but because he felt dirty. She was going to kiss him; Touch him, make love to him. And for the first time in six months. He didn't feel worthy. He felt worthless and unlovable.

Flawed
Track 8

Inspired by: Tryan Be

Q & A

Q: Wow, that's kind of fucked up. I can't believe you did that. Did you do it again after?

A: Man, trust me, I know. I really hate that I did it. And I hated the fact that I had done it again. It was just something about her... I mean, Erica that I couldn't let go of. And I messed up.

8

Chris had barely slept since the night Jasmine had shown up at his door and kissed him goodnight, completely unaware of what had happened just minutes before. She asked him why his place smelled funny, and he told her it was his gym clothes he needed to do laundry. She offered to do it for him, but he turned her down.

Chris would lie in bed most nights staring at the ceiling, the sound of her breathing next to him made him feel like he was stealing peace he didn't deserve. He couldn't eat around her, not while her family was over. Being face to face with her brother became an impossible task. Her little cousin, who used to make him laugh, now made him feel like a ghost in his own body. He told himself he'd never do it again.

But three days later, he went to Erica's place. His heart told him he was going to end it, that he needed to say it to her face *it's done. I'm in love with someone else.* But his body betrayed him. Right there in the doorway of her apartment.

"I love Jasmine. I can't do this with you, Erica." Erica smiled like she'd heard it all before.

"You came here to tell me that?" Her hands pressed against his zipper. "You took a cab all the way here for a goodbye?" He didn't answer.

Her hands unbuckled his belt. Her perfume snaked around him like a memory. She caressed him and said.

"That's not how you say goodbye." She moaned. He tried to fight it, but his body was weak. Weak to her touch. "You can have both," she whispered. "I won't say a word." And like a fool, a puny, selfish man, he let himself fall deep into her again. Each time he walked away from her place, he hated himself a little more than the last time.

The guilt bloomed like mold on his soul. He barely spoke when Jasmine asked about his day. She would ask him what was wrong, he would just blame it on the stress of his new position at work. He kept his phone flipped over all the time now. His phone, which would go off with hundreds of notifications, now sat with notifications off. Claiming it was too distracting when she asked. He felt like, if Jasmine hugged him long enough, she'd smell the lie clinging to his skin with a hint of Erica's perfume that lingered.

He tried to go cold on Erica.

No texts.

No calls.

But temptation isn't always a person; it's a pattern. And Chris was creating one. The fifth time it happened, he cried in the shower, realising he had lost control of the situation. He cried as if tears would rinse away his sins. Scrubbed her out of his fingertips. But it didn't work.

Jasmine called him one night just to say she missed him. And he couldn't even say "I love you" back without choking. He called Jackson in the morning, and they met in the park later that day. Chris sat on the bench, hoodie pulled low covering his eyes, and his hands nervously rubbed together.

"I fucked up, bro."

"You fuck up every week!" Jackson said casually.

"Nah," Chris looked up. "I fucked up for real." He told him everything. Not just the night of the dinner, but the days after. Before he even finished speaking.

"You told me she was different," Jackson said, disappointment written all over his face. Chris nodded, eyes riddled with guilt.

"She is."

"Why on earth would you do that to her? You stupid" Jackson could not hold back his judgment. Chris didn't answer. Telling Jackson the truth...that he didn't know why, that he couldn't fight the temptation, that he was afraid of his own feelings.

That it felt too good, too fast, too real would have completely broken him down.

In that moment, the fear of losing Jasmine became real.

What's Done In, The Dark... Track 9

Inspired by: Last Heartbreak Song

Q & A

Q: Not gonna lie, that's a shitty situation to be in. Did Jasmine ever find out?

A: Hell yeah she did ! She broke things off with me. That was the day my life changed forever.

9

The universe always has a way of revealing what it wants you to know, even if you didn't ask for it. Jasmine wasn't looking to uncover anything that day. But his paranoia led him to believe that a part of her knew what happened. They planned to watch movies together, and the pizza was on its way. When the neighbor came knocking, Chris sat back, and Jasmine opened the door. Mrs. Mary from down the hall had a package stolen and asked Jasmine if she could look at the camera. Jasmine walked back to get her phone. Chris asked her if everything was okay. She explained what was happening with the neighbor. Jasmine opened her phone.

"Ms. Mary, what day do you think they took it ?" She asked.

"I think it was last month; I've been waiting, "Ms. Mary responded. They said they delivered it, but I never received it."

"You're gonna have to give me a date and time so I can look at it," Jasmine explained.

Ms. Mary pulled out her phone and scrolled through her emails to find the delivery notice.

"They delivered it on Friday, March 28, at 6pm."

"Okay." Jasmine smiled. "That was the night of my cousin's rehearsal dinner, just about 3 weeks ago. I hope I still have the video."Chris' ears perked up. Jasmine scrolled to the date and time.

The scroll became more observant as she slowed down and looked. Both hands now on the phone, zooming in. Chris sat up nervously.

"Ms. Mary, I'm sorry, it didn't catch the thief." She lied.

"Thank you, Jasmine." She watched as Ms.Mary wobbled off mumbling about her missing package. Closing the door behind her, she looked disturbed.

"What the fuck is this? She turned her phone, with the video feed from her camera app facing him. Her fingers scrolled through the timeline. She watched him as he watched in shock. 11:58 p.m. clear as day, Chris walked with a girl to the front door; he kissed her. 12:05 a.m. Jasmine enters the building and takes the elevator.

"Who is that, Chris?" Chris doesn't respond as he searches for words. "You fucked me and her the same night." Tears rolled down her face as she remembered that night. How she kissed Chris on the couch. How he held; her like everything was fine. She stopped the video and sat there.

Silent.

Then she spat venom.

"You really fucked up. I trusted you. I fucking loved you." Chris sat still, not saying a word. When he finally spoke, he tried to explain.

"Please, Jazz, it's not what you think."

"You had a girl in my building," she said. "The same night we were at my cousin's dinner and you fucked her, did you not?"

"She showed up unexpectedly.

"You walked her out and kissed her and I saw it."

"We just talked Jazz, I swear."

"Just talked?" She said flatly. "Let me see your phone."

Chris hesitated. And in that pause, he lost her. She walked toward him, hand out. He gave it to her. She opened the message. Erica's name lit the screen. She didn't have to scroll far. There were pictures, messages, and time-stamps of link-ups. This Erica girl knew about her. She read messages saying, *How's ya little girlfriend doing?* Jasmine's hands trembled.

"I can explain, please!" He begged. "That night, she showed up, and."

"You fucked her." Jasmine said. "Didn't you? You fucked both of us."Chris stared at the floor."Didn't. You?"

"Yes," he finally revealed. The silence after that felt like death.

She nodded slowly, lips pressed tight as if...if she opened them, the rage would burst out of her.

"Get out."

"Jazz please."

"GET THE FUCK OUT!" she screamed. Chris didn't argue; He stopped begging.

He just walked past her, down the hallway, and out the door.

She closed the door, locking him out of her life.

Lie
Track 10

Inspired by: Lie Again

Q & A

Q: Damn! That's how she found out. Both on the same night, you wild fam. So after all of that, how do you feel about lying?

A: I fucked up so bad that I actually wanted her to lie to me. Because she was so honest. It hurt more than anything. She didn't sugarcoat shit. She didn't protect me from her truth. I was asking questions about things a really did not want the answers too.

10

He hadn't seen her in weeks, not really seen her. Just flashes across the street, ducking into a cab. Standing at the bodega, smiling politely at the guy behind the counter. Never at him. Not since she blocked him. Not since she told him to get out. The flowers he left at her door wilted. The sticky notes curled at the corners, untouched. She never even peeled them off. She left them to decay like the new version of his heart. The night he saw her again. She came out of the building in a soft brown hoodie, curls tucked into a beanie, laughing at something the guy in the car said. Chris stopped breathing.

She handed the guy in the car something through the window. A charger, maybe, or her heart. And then she climbed in. That moment cracked something wide open. Not just jealousy; No, jealousy would've been easier to manage. The grief made his chest ache from the inside. Seeing her with someone else meant it was real. She was trying. Trying to move on. Trying to find joy again. And she wasn't trying with him. He found himself back at her door without remembering how he got there.

The hallway was quiet. His legs folded beneath him. He sat still on the floor. He listened to the hum of the building. Thinking about everything he'd say if he had the chance, he rehearsed it, edited it, deleted it in his head. *I'm sorry*. Sounded too thin. *You were right*. Didn't feel like enough.

Come back to me. Felt wrong, and dishonest. And the worst part was, he still hadn't let Erica go completely. He hadn't seen her for days. He hadn't slept with her again. Hadn't even texted. But she was still there. Lingering and complicated. But she represented the pain he now had to live with. But Jasmine had never been easy. That's what made her unforgettable.

He was halfway through convincing himself to leave when he heard keys. Then footsteps. Then the door unlocked. She looked the same. Smelled the same. When her eyes landed on him, she froze. She didn't say a word. She didn't flinch. He stood. She turned her key, pushed the door open, and walked in without acknowledging him. But she left the door ope n.That was enough. He stepped inside, quietly shutting the door behind him. Her place smelled the same, cocoa-butter, vanilla, honey and warmth. The silence between them sat heavy. He could hear his own breath and heartbeat. Jasmine didn't offer him a seat. She didn't ask why he was here. She leaned against the edge of the kitchen counter, arms crossed, her stare burning a hole through him. Finally, she spoke.

"You don't get to do this."

"I had to see you."

"You did." Her voice was even."Now what?"

He hesitated.

"I miss you." She looked away, almost laughing, but not out of humor. More like disbelief.

"You miss what you ruined?"

"Jazz..."

She closed her eyes and winced at the nickname. But she didn't stop him."I made a mistake."

"Mistake?" Her voice cracked and then sharpened. "You had something real, and you let it rot. Chaos was your choice. You lied." Her breath caught as she said. "You...you broke every promise you made."

"I didn't mean to."

"But you did it; Anyway."

Chris couldn't look at her.

"I'm not trying with you anymore," she said. "I'm trying with me now."

He nodded slowly, every word slicing deeper than the last. "Are you seeing him?" He paused. He already knew the answer. But asking made it real."Yes."

"How long?"

"He is my ex if you must know. We reconnected two weeks ago"

"Is it serious?"

"Does it matter, Chris?"

"Of course it matters." Chris swallowed hard. "Why him?"

Jasmine looked him dead in the eye.

"He never cheated on me." Silence. That silence said everything. "He never stopped loving me." She added. "Even when I left."

Chris looked down at the floor, his throat tight. That was the dagger.

"I don't need the truth." He muttered, voice low, almost broken. "You could've kept that shit to yourself."

"I'm not you," she said. "I don't lie to people I love." That made him crumble. He nodded again, then again, as if it would make it hurt less. But it didn't.

"I'm sorry," he whispered. She said nothing. He turned toward the door, hand on the knob.

"Chris."He looked back."I hope you find someone who makes you tell the truth."His mouth cracked a smile, trying to mask his feelings.

"That was supposed to be you."

"I was. Until you made lying look easier." Her last words before he left.

Ghost
Track 11

Inspired by: Vanish

Q & A

Q: So what did life look like once you realized she wasn't coming back?

A: For weeks, I spiraled. I kept thinking I could fix it, that maybe if I gave her space, she'd come back. But we lived in the same building. Space wasn't real. Still, the distance she created felt like we lived in different countries. She disappeared, and her absence haunted the hallway.

11

Chris watched from his fifth-floor window, the same window where he used to wave at her coming home, where she used to blow him kisses before she made it inside. Now, he just watched. Below, Jasmine stepped out of the building. Her braids tucked beneath her blue Yankees fitted, hoodie loose, casual like always. Except she wasn't alone. The car was there again. Same guy. This time, he brought flowers. Chris clenched the curtain in his fist. She laughed at something. Touched the guy's arm before she got in. The car pulled away. She didn't look up. Inside, the apartment felt colder.

His phone rang. Erica.He stared at the name, then answered.

"Are you coming over later?" she asked. He paused.

"Nah! I'm busy." He wasn't. It wasn't the first time he had lied to Erica. The irony didn't escape him. He blamed her for all of it. But deep down, he knew. He blamed himself more. Still, he kept her around; Not out of love, not even out of lust, but out of habit, out of guilt. If he had let her go, it would all have been for nothing. He hated her. He hated what he'd done and who he was becoming.

He sat on the couch Jasmine used to fall asleep on. Her throw blanket still folded on the armrest, untouched. Her hair tie was still under the coffee table. He could see it from where he sat.

She erased him from her Instagram.

Every photo.

All the memories of them. Gone. Like he never existed. Like he was a ghost. Her words replayed constantly. "I'm not trying with you anymore. I'm trying with me now." It echoed louder every night. He called Jackson.

"Yo," Jackson answered.

"She's really gone, man."

Jackson remained quiet at first.

"You mean, like...done?" Chris nodded, even though Jackson couldn't see it.

"She blocked me. Deleted everything. Won't talk to me. I don't even exist anymore."Jackson exhaled.

"What'd you expect?" Chris didn't answer. "She was good for you, bro," Jackson finally said. "She made you soft. And that's not a bad thing."

Chris ran a hand over his face.

"I don't feel soft now. I feel hollow; A piece of me is missing, man."

Jackson sighed.

"Don't let her haunt you; You're already ghosting yourself."

Chris sat in the dark, phone on his chest, TV on mute.

No Erica.

No Jasmine.

Just silence as he ceases to exist in his own world.

Unblock Me
Track 12

Inspired by: Still Your Best

Q & A

Q: Emotionally, how did you feel?

A: My heart broke. Any time I could get from her, I took it. Just to get a slight opportunity again. Just to feel close to her. Even if it was fake. Even if she hated me for it. I needed something.

12

It was a little after 3 p.m. when Chris stepped out of his building to grab a pineapple soda and flirt with Oreo, the bodega cat, like he usually did when he needed to feel normal. Then he saw her. Jasmine, laughing and getting out of the passenger seat of a matte-black Camaro with gold rims and an IG handle tagged across the rear window like a brand. She looked happy; Her hair was different, pinned up and straight. The guy got out, too. He stood tall, like he owned the whole damn street. Designer sweats. Loud sneakers. Thick chain. Loud laugh, loud everything.

Chris froze mid-step, Oreo brushing past his ankle. He had never seen the guy in full like this. Not this close. But the second their eyes almost met, Chris looked away. He wasn't ready for that kind of mirror. Standing inside the bodega, he pulled out his phone like a reflex and opened Instagram. The handle was easy to find. He scrolled and saw nothing but cars.

Cars.

More cars.

Girls in cars.

Girls in bikinis posing next to cars.

Him; shirtless next to the same car. Caption: "Catch me if you can."

Chris's stomach turned. *This was the dude Jasmine left me for?* He paid for the soda and left quickly, the bottle sweating in his palm. His thoughts were messier than ever.

He was getting angry with his finger for scrolling. *This motherfucker is trash. That shit can't be real.* He zoomed in on his ugly- ass chain. *He's gonna cheat. Look at this shit. She must be blind if she doesn't see it.* He rushed back into his building, barely nodding at the maintenance man, and stomped up the stairs. By the time he reached his door, he was panting hard. Anger filled the surrounding air. He snatched a sticky note from his kitchen counter, grabbed a pen, and wrote.

Note
Unblock me. I have something to tell you.
Chris.

He walked down to Jasmine's floor, 1A, and stuck the note on her door like it was the last card in a game he was losing. Then he went back upstairs and waited. He stood by the window for what felt like forever, eyes locked on the street.

At 4:12 p.m. she came out and walked to the bodega. She paused. Look up at him as he watches her from his window. He saw when she read it; He saw the bright yellow paper in her hand. Chris's heart stopped. His hand gripped the windowsill. He watched her fingers move across her phone. He unlocked his phone.

Call, voicemail. Again, voicemail.

An hour passed. He called again

Text: Hi. Message not delivered.

He exhaled as if the wind had knocked him out. The next morning, his eyes opened before his alarm. 6:43 a.m. He sent another message; Can we talk? Message Delivered. His hands shook. He called again. No answer. But this time, it rang. Chris recorded a voice note.

<u>**Voice Note**</u>

"Jasmine, I know I hurt you. And I have to live with that. But I swear, I never want to see someone hurt you like that again. That guy he's not good for you. I know I'm not either, but. You deserve better than us. I'm here if you need me. Just know that I'm sorry. "

He hit send, hesitated, then sent another.

<u>**Voice Note**</u>

"He's a fuckboy, Jasmine. I can see it. I can smell it. You think I hurt you? He's gonna destroy you. I know I messed up. But how could you choose him over me? I was the best you ever had. You told me that. And you're still the best thing I've ever lost."

And then he waited.

Hopeful.

For The Streets
Track 13

Inspired by: Fields

Q & A

Q: Tell me the truth; How bad did you crash out?

A: Bro, I had a full-blown crash out. No cap. I messaged the dude. Shit got crazy.

13

There was a silence that felt like death. Jasmine didn't respond to the voice note; not the long ones, not the short ones, definitely not the desperate ones either. She didn't block him again, which made it worse. She left the door cracked but never opened it. Chris called. She answered.

"Look," he said, voice low, calm, like he was holding something volatile in his throat. "I'm not trying to stress you. I just think you need to know what's right in front of your face." Her silence was venomous.

"Then clearly I was blind, cause I didn't see the shit you were doing in front of mine."

That hit.

"It was a mistake." Chris murmured. "Because I wasn't over her. Erica. I should've told you that." The words tasted like rust. But it was the first time he'd been honest. Honest with himself. Honest with Jasmine. There was a shift in her tone. Not forgiveness, but maybe understanding.

"Yeah, well," Jasmine sighed. "I wasn't over him either. Clearly, I went back too."

That moment cracked something open.

They kept talking.

Slowly. Not flirting, not forgiving, just talking. And to Chris, that was everything. A breath of oxygen in the middle of him drowning. So he spiraled. Hope made him reckless.

That night, he made a burner account. He messaged Jasmine's new man, ex, whatever you wanna call him.

Message

Chris: Yo! Stop messing with Jasmine. She's not for you.

He stared at the screen, heart thudding in his chest like a riot.

Three dots popped up. Then a reply.

Car dude: Who the fuck are you?

Chris never responded. He couldn't, already feeling the shame hot on his neck. He knew he had crossed a line. But it was too late. The next day, his phone rang. Jasmine. He answered quickly.

"Are you out of your fucking mind?" She barked, fury cracking through every syllable. "Why would you do that?"

"What are you talking about?"

"Don't play with me, Chris. You know exactly what I'm talking about."

"I really don't."

"You messaged my boyfriend. Stop messing with Jasmine. Nobody else would say that. Nobody but you. What if he was crazy, Chris, you don't fucking think?" Chris's breath caught.

"You're right, I am sorry," he finally said. I know you don't love him. You're just doing this to hurt me. And it's working. Okay? Jasmine, you won, just stop. Can't you see I am fucked up about you? Let's! just try to work things out, please."

"Chris."

"No! Listen, stop pretending. Getting under someone to get over me is crazy...You know we're not done. You know this isn't it for us. You're supposed to be with me. Not some fast-ass car clown."

Jasmine went silent. Chris kept going. "You look stupid with him, thinking you're hurting me? You're hurting yourself. Playing yourself out here trying to prove a point. You're walking through these streets with wolves, thinking you're untouchable."

Still silent. Then.

Click!

She hung up. Chris stood in the middle of his apartment, sweating, panting, fists clenched, heart racing. He opened his messages. Typed.

<u>Text</u>

Chris : Stop fucking with that dude.

Message delivered, but no reply. He stood there, phone in hand, watching the void stare back at him. And in that moment, Chris realized he was the wolf he tried to warn her about, the one she walked away from.

I Miss You, But...
Track 14

Inspired by: Let Me Go

Q & A

Q: It seemed likely that before you crashed out, she might have been willing to forgive you?

A: She did. She accepted my apology, understanding that neither of us was over our exes. So we stayed cool. But I didn't want to be cool. I wanted her.

14

Chris couldn't manage a "just friends" relationship with Jasmine. Not when her voice still sounded like home. Not when she started texting back again. She didn't unblock him all at once. First it was Instagram, then Snapchat. Then came the random check-ins; *"What* are you *doing? Did you finish the project?"* Simple things, nothing flirty. But it meant everything. To Chris, it meant maybe. She even let him stop by once or twice. Quick visits. Sitting at opposite ends of her couch like strangers who used to be something else. Watching whatever was on TV but not really paying attention. Silence did most of the talking. And he told himself; If she were really done, she wouldn't let him in at all. That lie kept him going. So he stayed close. Close enough to touch, even if he didn't. Close enough to hope. Jasmine never said she wanted him back. But she didn't tell him to leave, either. And that was enough for Chris to imagine it wasn't really over. Until it was.

They were sitting in her kitchen, drinking orange soda like old times, when he said it.

"I miss us."

Jasmine looked up from her cup.

"Chris..."

"I miss you. Us, before all this, before the lies, before Erica, before I fucked up. I miss how it was when it was just you and me."

Her face softened for a second, like maybe she missed it too. But she held her ground.

"We said we'd be cool." She responded.

"I don't wanna be cool. I want you."

She blinked slowly.

"So... what are you saying?"

Chris hesitated. "I'm saying this...this in-between shit hurts. You either take me back, or..."

She raised her eyebrows. "Or what..? Are you trying to give me an ultimatum?"

He paused. The words cut deep. "What? No."

"Let me be clear, Chris. Because I don't want to assume. Are you saying be with you... or lose you as a friend?"

Chris's throat tightened. That wasn't what he wanted to say, but maybe that was what he meant. He was tired of pretending. Of being near her and acting like he didn't want to hold her hand. Or kiss her. Or erase the past so they could move forward with their future. He wanted all of her or none. But he knew if he said that, she might pick none. So he looked away. Looked down at his hands.

"Never mind."

Jasmine nodded slowly, almost as if she expected it. "Oh, okay."

They sat there for another minute in that hollow space between love and letting go.

Then, Jasmine got up and started rinsing out her cup.

Chris stayed seated, knowing the silence between them said more than anything else.

Slow Down
Track 15

Inspired by: Take Time

Q & A

Q: So what happened after the ultimatum?

A: I took a shot in the dark because I wasn't gonna let her go.

15

Chris didn't linger. He knew Jasmine was going out with her girls; he saw the heels lined up by the door and the make-up bag sitting on the counter. This wasn't the night to press. So when she hugged him lightly, he didn't hold on too long. He didn't question the moment. Didn't beg. He just nodded, whispered, Goodnight. His barely touched orange soda sat forgotten on her counter. He took the elevator back up to his floor. Back in his apartment, he sat on the edge of his bed. Phone beside him. Elbows on knees. Face in hands.

"You almost fucked it all up." He muttered to himself. The ultimatum nearly slipped. The weight of it still sat heavy in his chest. But he didn't say it. And maybe, just maybe, that saved something. He looked across the room at the door. Thought about the sticky note she had left him months ago. The first one. The yellow square that changed everything. Her handwriting, slanted and soft. It wasn't just paper. It was hope. And maybe if he gave her space, a gesture, a choice she'd respond in kind. He picked up his phone and recorded a voice note. No rehearsal. Just raw.

<u>Voice Note</u>

"I love you. Every part of me loves you. I know you set your boundaries, and I swear I've tried to respect them, but... I can't. I don't want to. I want to show up for you, Jazz. Even if it's small. Even if I'm not the guy. I just need to be in the room. If there's still a door open... leave me a note. Just like before. I'll be up. I'll wait."

He exhaled, pressed send.Then walked to his front door, smoothed out a fresh sticky note, and wrote one sentence:

<u>Note</u>

If you're willing to let me love you leave something here.

He stuck it dead center on his door. And he waited.

Next To You
Track 16

Inspired by: For Tonight

Q & A

Q: So... did you get a note on your door?
A: I got something.

16

The room was dark except for the flicker of the screen. Chris sat motionless on the couch, game controller in hand, headset wrapped around his head, the glow of the TV casting dim flashes across his face. He played the football game, but his mind was nowhere near it.

"You think she's gonna respond?" Jackson asked through the headset.

Chris let out a quiet breath. "I don't know, bro. I hope she does. But I'm not expecting anything anymore. I'm humbled, whatever happens. I'll take it."

Silence passed between plays.

Then.

A knock; subtle, but unmistakable. Chris froze. His thumb hovered over the controller. He pushed the headset off one ear.

"What was that?" Jackson said. Chris didn't answer. His eyes shifted toward the door. Another knock; harder but hesitant. Jackson's voice came again. "It's 1 a.m. dawg. Who the hell's at your door this late? Oh shit, is that..."

Chris's heart pounded.

"I think...I think it's Jasmine."

He paused the game, dropping the controller on the floor.

"I'll call you back," he blurted before disconnecting Jackson. He was already moving. He opened the door and saw her. She was walking away down the hallway slowly, shoulders tight, hoodie pulled over her head like she was trying to hide from the world. She held her arms across her chest.

"Jasmine."

She stopped and turned around. Her eyes glistened, red and wet. Chris didn't wait. He moved toward her with urgency. When he reached her, she broke. No words just tears. And then, like gravity itself cracked open, she collapsed into him. He caught her, holding her like she might slip through his arms if he loosened his grip.

"Come on," he whispered. He lifted her. Carried her the way he always imagined he'd carry her across a threshold, except this wasn't joy. This was something more fragile. He brought her inside and gently kicked the door closed behind them. Treating her like glass, he gently lowered her onto the couch. She said nothing. She looked down, avoiding his eyes. Chris knelt in front of her.

"What happened?"

"I still love you," she said. Her voice cracked. "And I'm confused."

He reached up and wiped her tears with his thumb. They sat there in stillness for a moment. The room was soft and light, with memories of their happiness floating around the room.

Then, Jasmine looked up at him. And kissed him. He didn't resist her; he just kissed her like a promise... not one he was making, but one he was trying to keep. He knew this kiss was leading to something more, and he was ready. When the kiss broke, he searched her eyes.

"Are you sure?"

"Yes." She said, She stood, took his hand. And led him into the bedroom. No words passed between them as they stood facing each other in the low, warm light. She reached for the zipper of her hoodie. He reached for the zipper of his hoodie. One by one, they removed layers.

Shirt.

Undershirt.

Jeans.

Socks.

Silence. The silence created space between them. They stood there bare, observing each other. They saw each other fully for the first time in a long time. And then they stepped into each other's arms. There was no; Music, just skin, just memory and what crashing into forgiveness feels like. They made love as though the world had fallen away. Like nothing existed but the two of them.

Jasmine's hand slid over his shoulder like it knew the shape of him. Chris kissed her like he was remembering what home tasted like. There was no rush. They moved together on the bed, bodies tangled under a blanket. The memory of her warmth devoured him. When it was over, they didn't speak. They just stayed like that, holding each other. Wrapped in their past but stuck in the moment.

For once, there was no guilt or confusion to be made. No lies or distance between them.

Just them. Tonight, she was next to him. And he didn't ask what it meant. Why would he?

Because tonight was enough, it was the hope he waited for.

Talk
Track 17

Inspired by: Like I Want You

Q & A

Q: I was not expecting that. What happened after?
  A: Nothing I wanted.

17

Chris woke up alone. The space beside him was cold. Jasmine was gone. No kiss, no goodbye. Just the imprint of her presence that lingered in his sheets. He lay there staring at the ceiling, arms folded behind his head, trying to replay the night in his mind like a film he didn't want to end. This was the night he had waited for. He felt the night would change everything. But all he had now was an empty bed. He got up slowly, bare feet brushing the floor. In the kitchen, the morning light cast long shadows through the blinds. He opened the fridge to get a bottle of water, and that's when he saw it.

A sticky note. Neatly placed. Written in her familiar handwriting.

Note

We need to talk. Coffee shop, 2 p.m.

- Jazz

He stared at it for a long time. This wasn't the note he wanted. Not after last night. Not after everything. He checked his phone. 1:30 p.m. Panic settled in his nervous system. He brushed his teeth. Threw on jeans and a hoodie. Rushed out the door. Down the stairs. Through the city he didn't see. He made his way up the narrow staircase to the coffee shop, the one on the corner, with the big circle window. The same one from what felt like another lifetime. There she was, Jasmine, sitting at her favorite table by the round window. The sunlight hit her just right. Her face still, eyes unreadable.

She wasn't drinking coffee. She wasn't doing anything. Just staring out at the city, arms folded like she was bracing herself. Chris strolled toward her. "Hey!" he said. She stood and gave him a hug. It was soft. Polite but distant. He sat across from her.

"Do you want anything?" he asked. She shook her head no.

"No, I'm good."

That was unlike her. She always ordered something...an oat milk latte, with something sweet on the side. That's how he knew this would not be a light conversation and definitely not about them getting back together. She looked at him, steady, and said.

"Last night can't happen again."

His heart dropped. "What do you mean?"

"It was a mistake, Chris," she said." I shouldn't have done that because I was drunk and confused. I'm sorry."

Chris stared at her. At her lips. Her eyes. The light in her eyes was gone. He wanted to fight it. But she looked like someone already halfway out the door.

"I understand," he said, though he didn't. Inside, he was breaking. "Do you love him?" he asked.

She hesitated, then nodded. "I do."

He bit his lip, looked away, blinked back whatever was trying to form behind his eyes. Then he said it.

"I love you."

She sat still.

"Do you love Erica?" She asked.

"No!" he blurted. "I can't love her. I never did. She was a mistake. You're the only person I've ever actually loved."

Jasmine looked down at her hands.

"It can't happen again." She whispered as she stood up. He didn't stop her. She walked toward the stairs, and he sat frozen in that chair by the circle window. Watching, hoping for something, anything, to stop her. She reached the street and paused. Looked up. Their eyes met through the glass. Then she turned. And kept walking. A single tear fell from Chris's eye as he sat there, alone. Watching her literally walking out of his life.

No Eye Contact
Track 18

Inspired by: Lost Me

Q & A

Q: Damn... that would've had me so fucked up. How did you function?

A: Honestly, I just started fucking anything. I was not myself.

18

Chris sat in the coffee shop long after Jasmine left. Everyone in the coffee shop kept moving. But none of it felt the same. His heart had been holding on to a dream, but now all he had left was an empty seat. He called Jackson while staring out the window.

"What's good, bro?" Jackson answered, voice light.

Chris fought back the cracks in his voice before he responded.

"She said It can't happen again." he finally muttered. "Like last night was nothing. A mistake."

Jackson paused.

"Damn. You good?"

"Naw bro, shit got me fucked up. Literally, I can't even bring myself to get up."

"Don't trip. Where are you?

"I am up the block in the coffee shop"

"Give me 10 minutes; I'll come scoop you after this delivery.

"I am here, bro." Chris said, voice flat.

"Bet! We're gonna hit the spot, you're gonna forget about that shit by morning. Jackson's voice sounded elated. "We out"

"Later, bro."

"Cool!" Jackson ended the call.

By 9 p.m., they were at a bar near Atlantic. Loud music, shots lined up like coping mechanisms, and two women laughing harder than they needed to. Jackson did most of the talking. Chris nodded, smiling when he had to. The girl dancing with him was pretty enough. Long lashes, a nice body. She was grinding against him to the music; She didn't even ask his name, just took his hand and led him past the crowd. Into the hallway and into the bathroom. She locked the door behind them. Then she dropped to her knees. Chris didn't look down. He leaned back against the wall, eyes on the ceiling, letting it happen. She pleased him until her mouth filled. She swallowed and then wiped her mouth when she finished. He zipped his pants. Walked out without a word. She didn't stop him. She didn't speak. Neither did he.

By 12:08 a.m. He was standing outside Erica's door. He knocked once. She opened. No hesitation. She smiled when she saw him, relief on her face, arms already reaching for his shoulders. She kissed him. He barely kissed her back.

"So... what's up?" he said, voice low.

Erica didn't answer with words. She lifted her shirt and bent herself over the couch, facing away from him. Then she said. "So what's up?"

Chris closed the door and walked over. He tugged her panties down, unzipped his pants, and started. No eye contact. Erica was just a place for him to release. Just another body, he felt, with no emotions. When it was over, she turned to him, eyes gazing softly at him. She wanted to have more of him, like she still. Chris got up and started putting on his clothes.

"You're not staying?" she asked.

"I can't, I have to work in the morning." He put on his shoes by the door and then told her to close it on his way out, and that was that. Chris didn't sleep that night. Just stared at his ceiling, feeling everything he was trying to numb crawl back under his skin. By morning, missed calls and unread messages loaded his phone. He ignored them all. Until night fell again. He was back at Erica's place. This is who he'd become now.

A man who is no longer looking for love, just someone he could call at midnight.

Straight To Voicemail
Track 19

Inspired by: When It's All Said and Done

Q & A

Q: Not gonna lie, that got dark. So you finally got to close the chapter?

A: Not really.

19

It had been two weeks. Fourteen full days since Jasmine had walked out of the coffee shop and out of his life again. He tried, he really did. Not in the ways he used to. He didn't stand outside her door, didn't leave sticky notes just to get her attention. And that was the hardest part. Because they still lived in the same building. Passing her door on his way to the elevator, he didn't stop anymore. Chris got his mail only at midnight, trying to avoid running into her at the mailbox. He ignored his thought, thinking it was her coming to him when he heard footsteps outside his door. Chris stopped his impulse to knock on her door late at night. He never called out to her when he saw her from the window. He gave her space. And the space became his prison. At his desk, fingers limp on the keyboard, Chris stared at nothing. The office moved on without him; phones rang, meetings started, jokes landed, but he wasn't really there. His mind was running in loops. He swallowed down the ache and opened his phone. Her name still saved as, Jasmine with heart emojis. He tapped it.

Call, no answer.

He waited.

Called again, straight to voicemail. That's when he knew. She wasn't just not picking up. She was choosing to ignore him. He stared at the screen for a long minute, then hit the record button.

<u>Voice Note</u>

"I just wanna say I get it. I've tried to stay away, Jazz. I've tried to give you space. But I can't not have you in my life.

You don't talk to me. I don't see you anymore. And maybe that's how it's supposed to be.

But I want you. I want you in my life, even if I can't have you. I'll take anything."

He didn't listen back. Just hit send. Then he locked his phone, leaned back in his chair, and stared at the ceiling, like maybe she'd be waiting for him up there. But she wasn't. An hour went by slowly. And still, she didn't respond.

One More Time
Track 20

Inspired by: Favorite Mistake

Q & A

Q: Don't leave me hanging, bro. What happened?

A: Shit everything and nothing happened at the same damn time.

20

It had been just a little over two hours since Chris had sent the voice note. No reply, no sign she even listened. He was sitting in his office, headphones off, eyes blank, staring at his computer he hadn't touched. The only thing moving was his knee, bouncing restlessly. Then, a message; Jasmine.

<u>Text</u>

Come over.

That was it. No emoji. No follow-up. Chris stared at the screen, then reached for his phone and called Jackson. He didn't even say hello.

"Yo, I sent her a voice note," he blurted, "and I didn't know if she was gonna respond. I was like, damn, maybe I shouldn't have even sent it; maybe I should've just let her go, right? But I couldn't just I don't know. I told her she had to be a part of my life, even if it was just a piece of her. And guess what she says? She texts me back. Just now. You know what she said?"

Jackson remained quiet, just letting him talk. "She said. 'Come over.' That's it; just come over. And I don't know what the fuck that even means, man. Like, is that her way of saying she heard me? Or is it just a booty call? Am I tripping? What the fuck am I supposed to do with that?"

Jackson finally spoke. "Bro, fuck that, are you serious right now?"

"I know how it sounds." Chris let out a dry scoff.

"She got a whole man. And she told you it was a mistake. She didn't even let you explain shit." Jackson rebutted. "And now she says, come over like y'all been good this whole time? That's wild."

Rubbing his eyes, Chris said. "You're not wrong when you're right, bro."

Jackson didn't have to say more. Chris said what they both knew.

"Yeah... I'm not going."

But as soon as the line went dead, Chris knew he was lying. He paced around his office a few times, then he grabbed his phone to text her.

<u>**Text**</u>

Chris: I'll be there by 4.

Jasmine replied seconds later.

Jasmine: Are you taking the train or a cab?

He blinked.

Chris: Do you need me?

Jasmine: Yes.

He swallowed hard.

Chris: Alright. I'll take a cab.

Thirty minutes later, Chris was standing in front of her door. The energy was different. He didn't even knock. The door opened before his hand touched it. She had been waiting. She kissed him softly at first. Then, hungrier, as if his lips were food, she would have devoured him. He pulled back.

"Jasmine... wait... What is this?"

She looked at him.

"Don't act like you don't want this."

"I do," he admitted. "But are we really not gonna talk?"

She stepped back, pulled her shirt over her head, and said.

"There's nothing to talk about right now. You need to be deep in this pussy."

He didn't say another word. This was a side of Jasmine he had never seen before. Maybe if he had seen her like this sooner, he wouldn't have been so thirsty for Erica.

His clothes hit the floor by the door. Hers followed. They moved together fast, hands catching skin, breath uneven. She pulled him toward the bedroom with urgency. They fell into bed like a bad habit. But love wasn't in the room. It was too physical. Hollow even. And for the first time, Chris felt it . He felt the way he treated Erica. His body was present. But the rest of him was somewhere far away. She turned away from him afterward, back to silence.

He kissed her shoulder once and got up.

"I gotta head upstairs," he said. "I've got some work to finish."

"Okay," she replied without looking. He got dressed and didn't speak a word. Before he left, he kissed her just once, just gently on the forehead, as she lay in bed. That was the only difference between what just happened and with Erica. That single kiss expressed compassion and longing.

He stepped into his apartment and closed the door behind him. Then leaned against it. And sank. All of it was hitting him now. *She didn't tell me she missed me. Didn't even say I loved you. She just wanted to fuck. That's all she needed me for.* And maybe that would've been enough if he hadn't begged for any piece of her. But now he realized he'd asked for the wrong thing. He'd told her he'd take anything, but now that he had, he felt disposable and used. The spiral wasn't just physical anymore; it was mental. He sat on his couch, fully dressed, unable to move.

He didn't know how to feel, and that scared him.

Again
Track 21

Inspired by: Stuck On You

Q & A

Q: Jackson was right. Y'all are both fucked up. But why did you lie to him?

A: I lied to Jackson because he was right. And if I told him I was gonna see her, I'd be the one putting the knife in my back. I couldn't stand causing myself pain. That's why I lied. He was the mirror I didn't want to look into.

21

There had been silence between them since that night. No texts, calls, no how you doing? Nothing. Chris had told himself that it was a good thing. Maybe it was over. He wouldn't let her use him again... that he'd learned. Then she texted him.

Text

Jasmine: Can you come down? I need to talk to you.

He hesitated and thought about calling Jackson for a second opinion about a complex decision. He wanted to flip his lucky coin for guidance once more. But that might tell him not to go. And that wasn't what he wanted. And just like that, he was standing in front of her door again. Jasmine opened it; nothing had happened no kiss, nothing. She was smiling. The air between them didn't carry the weight it usually did. It was light, calm, but dangerously comfortable.

They sat on the couch and talked like they were still friends, like none of it had happened, and all of it did. Chris raised an eyebrow.

"You're chipper today." He tried to keep the mood light, not knowing what to expect at the moment.

Jasmine grinned. "Third cup of coffee. Kinda vibrating through time right now."

He laughed. She laughed. It all felt real again. And then she went quiet.

"I just want to apologize, Chris," she said. "For that night. For how I handled it. I think I want to be with you. I just don't know how."

He turned toward her, their knees brushing.

"You don't have to know how yet. Just say yes to us . Right now, this moment. That's all I want. Not sex, just you."

She looked at him. Really looked at him. And he kissed her; She kissed back. But it didn't stay soft for long. Jasmine pulled back and murmured.

"I'm leaving soon."

He paused and asked.

"Where?"

She shook her head.

"I'll tell you later."

Chris gave her a boyish smirk.

"Good thing I'm here, then. Let me give you something to remember before you leave."

He slid her pants down. She leaned back into the cushions. He pulled her legs over his shoulders and kissed her inner thighs, slow and deliberate as if he was reading scripture. His hands found her waist, then her throat lightly, then firmly he squeezed. Her head fell back, and eyes rolled. He didn't speak. But between her legs, he spoke another language. This wasn't about power or possession. This was about worship. It was about giving her what he hadn't been able to give anyone else since her.

Himself.

When it was done, he climbed up her body with his lips and kissed her deeply. Each kiss tasted like everything he still couldn't say out loud. She brushed her fingers against his face.

"I need to go pack," she whispered.

"Okay," he said, still dazed.

"Okay," she said as she kissed him.

He got dressed. She walked with him to the door. He stood at the door, not wanting to leave but knowing he had to go. With silence between them. His eyes locked with hers just before they kissed one more time before he walked away in pure bliss. He took the stairs two at a time, heart beating fast, soul still buzzing. Upstairs, Chris collapsed on his bed and smiled into the dark. He didn't tell Jackson. He wasn't ready to be judged. It would only undermine how he felt now. His energy peaked with maybes; maybe, just maybe, they were finally finding their way back to each other.

Feeling alive again, he slept peacefully, dreaming of her.

Hopeful of what was yet to come.

Gone
Track 22

Inspired by: Heartbreak Anniversary

Q & A

Q: Did you get your girl back?
  A: Yeah. That's what I thought.

22

Chris woke up with a smile still lingering from the night before. The memory of her laughter. The curve of her neck under his lips. It replayed in his mind like a scene he planned to revisit forever. He sat up, rubbed his eyes, and reached for his phone.

Text

Chris: You never told me where you were going.

Sent, but the message didn't deliver.

He stared at the screen.

Chris: Jazz?

Again. Message not delivered. He checked the time: 1:45 p.m. He checked his signal. He had full service. A puzzled look emerged on his face. He tried calling again, but a message played. *"Your call cannot be completed as dialed. Please check the number and try again."*

"What the fuck?"

He redialed. Same message.

Third time.

Fourth.

His breath caught in his chest.

He opened Instagram. Typed her name.

Nothing.

Snapchat! Gone.

TikTok! Deleted.

He opened WhatsApp, desperate. He messaged. His last hope was a blue checkmark. But she wasn't there either.

She had erased herself. *But not from the apartment.* He thought. He paused at his door and questioned. *She couldn't have left, not that fast. Not without saying goodbye. Not after last night.* He flew down the stairs, skipping two at a time, heart thudding in his chest like a warning bell. He tried to suppress his intrusive thoughts. *What if that's what she meant when she said she was leaving?*

Standing at her door.

Frozen, staring at it. As if he could see through the wood and get answers. He lifted his hand and knocked hard. The door creaked open under the force. He stepped inside. The apartment was empty and still. Couch remained, a rug and the frog mug she broke months ago sat on the counter. The soul of the apartment was gone. He walked through the space slowly. He was now trespassing in a nightmare. No sneakers stacked against her wall. The stand where she kept her hat collection was empty. He opened her bedroom door. The dresser that kept her vanilla oils and perfume was clutter-free. The bathroom cabinet was cleared out. Closets had only hangers.

And then he saw it. On the shelf by the window, the one she decorated with family pictures and candles. Sitting was the teddy bear. The one he gave her on their first date. The one with the tiny sneakers. It stared back at him like a ghost of everything they could've been. Chris didn't cry right away.

He just stood there, arms limp, breath caught in his throat. And then it came. The tears rolled down his face. They poured down hot and slow as he stood in the quiet of her apartment. Then he collapsed onto the couch the; Same one he'd laid her on last night. He stared into the emptiness.

"Was it all fake?"

"Did she ever love me?"

"Was I just the backup plan, the convenient body, the person she went to when her real life didn't feel right?

He wiped his face with his sleeve, stood up, and looked around one more time.

No goodbye. The bear that never asked to be left behind.

This was a day he would never forget. Not her birthday, not their first kiss. It would be this day. The day after she told him she wanted him. How he believed her. The day she disappeared. The day that changed him forever.

Damaged
Track 23

Inspired by: Scarred

Q & A

Q: I'm sorry it played out like that. How did you recover from that?

A: Thanks! I'm still in recovery. It feels like PTSD but with love. PTLD. I'm forever changed, and I can't tell you if it's for better or worse.

23

Chris didn't tell Jackson. He couldn't. There was no way to explain what it felt like to wake up full and go to bed hollow. No words for what it meant to be left with nothing but a teddy bear and silence. And if he said it out loud, if he said that Jasmine vanished like smoke the day after they made love, it would sound like fiction. Like a man exaggerating his heartbreak to win sympathy.

So he kept it to himself. Erica was the only person left. She was always there waiting like a puppy at the door, ears perked, tail wagging, loyal beyond reason.

He showed up at her place without warning.

She let him in without asking questions. They sat in silence. Her eyes watched him, trying to read his mood. But Chris wasn't there to talk. He was there to forget. And that's what he did. He didn't kiss her. Not really. Not like before. His hands moved the same way, but there was no intention behind them. Just memory and muscle. His body did the loving, but his heart stayed packed in a box somewhere in Jasmine's now-vacant room. Afterward, he stood to leave. That's when Erica spoke.

"I know things have been off... and I know it's been a few months since you and Jasmine ended," she said softly, "but I want more. I want us to be something."

Chris blinked at her. Confused as if she were speaking a language he no longer understood.

"Erica," he said flatly, "I told you... I'm not doing that relationship shit right now."

She swallowed, blinking back tears. "But... why not? We've been good. Haven't we?"

"We've been fucking," he said. "That doesn't make us good."

Her bottom lip quivered.

"I just want more. I want you."

Chris grabbed his hoodie and shook his head.

"I can't give you that."

She reached out and grabbed his arm.

"Please don't go. You don't have to love me. I'm not asking for that. I just... I don't want to be alone tonight."

Something in her voice small, crumpled, desperate made him pause. He sat back down.

She curled onto his side, sighing as if she'd won. Like she was safe. Her body folded into him like home. But he didn't hold her.

He didn't kiss her forehead.

He didn't play with her hair

He just sat there breathing, blinking, hollow. She didn't know it, but she'd never have him. Not the way Jasmine did. That version of Chris was gone. Lost in a moment that felt like forever but only lasted one night.

And now?

Now he was a void. Existing only as proof that something once hurt him.

It's All Good
Track 24

Inspired by: Unholy Matrimony

Q & A

Q: Wow! You were so detached. Did it help you in the long run ?

A: For a while I was numb, just coasting, you know. But it all caught up with me. And I couldn't run from myself anymore .

24

Chris sat on the edge of his bed, one foot on the ground, the other dangling. A sock half-on, half-off. For the first time in a long time; He didn't have the music blasting to distract him from his feelings. Just him, and the silence he tried so long to avoid. He stared at the floor, eyes focused, even though mind wandered. *Where did I go wrong?* That was the question tonight. Not *why did she leave? Was it worth it?* Just; *Where did I fuck up?* He hadn't really asked himself that. And now, finally still, the answers crept in like light that crept through an open door. He cheated on Jasmine. That part was obvious. But it wasn't just about sex; It was about control. About fear. About needing to be wanted but afraid to be known. With Jasmine, there were parts of himself he never exposed. Desires, thoughts, urges pieces he buried. *Why couldn't he open up to her?*

Why didn't he trust her with his whole being?

Did that mean he didn't love her? Or did it mean... he did. That terrified him. He pressed his palm to his chest. That fear it didn't come out of nowhere. It came from him. From watching his father. A rigid man. A soldier, even when he wasn't in uniform. He was predictable, like the wash cycle; Wake up, work, home; Repeat never missing a bill or a beat. But always... distant. His mother waited at home, lonely and in misery, hoping for more than a man focused on duty and routine. Eventually, she gave up.

Her giving up would shatter his family forever. The day his father found out that his mother was unfaithful. Was a day he wished he had never been present for.

Chris remembered that night clearly his father coming home crying. For the first time, he saw a grown man cry. Chris had woken up from the noise. He stood outside his parents' door, too afraid to go in. He had heard his mother's complaints about not being happy. Then she demanded a divorce. Sobbing, his father stormed out of the room. He didn't even notice that Chris was at the door. Chris had never seen a man cry like that. Hadn't known it was possible. Chris crawled into bed with his mother to comfort her and himself. Later that night; His father came back, banging on the door.

"Please, let me in." His father had stood outside pounding on the front door like the house.

With each knock came the sound of thunder. Chris was scared but his mother didn't flinch; Didn't move. Just stared out the window once, then went back to bed. Chris begged his mother on behalf of his father.

"Can Daddy come inside?"

"Go to sleep." She said as she tucked him in. And that was it. By morning, the cops were at the door.

"Ma'am , we're sorry to inform you that your husband, Christopher Ellis Sr. was involved in a fatal car crash late last night. Paramedics pronounced him dead at the scene."

Chris later found out his father was the drunk driver who critically injured 5 people and killed himself.

His father's death left him with something no child should know: the understanding that weakness will break you, love will break you. So he built armor, toughened his skin, made jokes instead of confessing, and cheated when fear prevented commitment.

Jasmine got the version of him that was still hiding. He told her he wanted forever. Talked weddings, futures, white dresses, and last names. But when the commitment came close, really close, he backed away. Not because she wasn't enough. But because she was more than enough. He knew he wasn't enough for her. Deep down, he doubted someone like her could love someone like him, if she knew what hid below the surface.

He remembered the night they talked about marriage, how he smiled and nodded. But inside, he panicked. The echo of his father crying came flooding back. *Was he becoming him?*

Or worse *was he becoming his mother?*

Chasing something she couldn't even name. Brave enough to walk away, too blind to see what she already had. Hungary, enough to want more from life.

Maybe that's what Chris had done too. And now, sitting here in this silence, his sock halfway on, heart closed, he finally admitted the thing he'd been dodging since Jasmine walked away.

I didn't lose her because she left.

I lost her because I never really let her in.

End Of It
Track 25

Inspired by: At Least We Tried

Q & A

Q: In losing Jasmine...what did you learn about letting love go?

A: That I hadn't really faced it before. Not fully. Losing Jasmine made me reflect on losing my father. And once I started untangling that, I realized I'd been grieving both of them at the same time. One was taken from me. The other walked away. But the pain felt the same. And I think, for the first time, I let myself feel it without numbing it, without running.

Q: What happened between you and Erica?

A: She got married. I used to think she wasted my time, or that I wasted hers. But honestly? I think she gave me love

I didn't know I needed. My inability to love her the way she needed to be loved is something I wish I could take back. I'm happy for her now because she found the love she deserved.

Q: Did you ever run into Jasmine again?

A: No, and I don't want to. And I don't say that with bitterness; it's my peace. For a long time, I needed answers. I needed to know if she was okay. If she missed me. If I crossed her mind. But now? I am good on that. I don't need to know anymore. That is the one thing I am sure of, for sure .

Behind The Mixtapes
Bonus Track 26

Author's story

Q & A

Q: For those of you wondering, why did I write this book?

A: The simple answer is that I was gonna write about my own dating life. But then I got nervous. I didn't want to let people into my life. It felt intrusive. But the idea never left me, and I wanted to share it. The fear of missing out, and the possibility that someone else had the same concept, scared me. So yeah, I scared myself into writing it. But, in the process, it made me want to share my story. I felt like I was Chris and Jasmine. As a friend, I am Jackson. I have treated people like Erica and have been treated like Erica. So continue to read, and you will find yourself immersed into my dating life and laughing at my corny jokes. I hope at the end of this, you reflect on your own dating life. To the ones who have loved and lost, and to the ones not afraid to love again.

Is It me? Am I The Toxic One?

So I'm gonna start this off just like any other millennial, trying to figure out what dating is after the fall of R&B. The title is pretty obvious, but trust me, the stories are juicy, so stick around. I am very dramatic, so if you're reading this and we dated or hooked up, just know I may or may not be adding a little razzle-dazzle. I won't say any names.

I became familiar with GIVĒON after hearing "Heartbreak Anniversary". My first thought was, *Damn, I feel bad for him who hurt you? He seemed like a good guy.* But then I kept listening and got hit with the ultimate level of toxicity. I started to overdose on his music. Shortly after that, I started to feel like he was my guide in the dating field, giving me advice on how to avoid men with this level of ain't shit-ness.

As I write this, sitting in my Savage X Fenty oversized onesie, braless with my melons dangling, drinking a low-calorie 0% alcohol Heineken, talking to my friends in Clubhouse a week before my 35th birthday I realize.

This is somewhat a true.

Not-so-true.

I-am-lying-out-my-ass.

Why-are-you-in-my-business. But I'm being honest while I lie to you. But mostly true. Kinda story.

Pumpkin pie

Let's start with Lost Me, my interpretation of this song and the relation-shit it's attached to. Maybe I'll add something I learned. Maybe not. This is just a timeline of events, and you're here for the ride. Now, let me paint you a picture of this rollercoaster. Imagine a person knowing they ain't shit but still trying to get with you just because it's fun for them. They give zero to no fucks about your feelings. The intensity of how things started would make anyone think it would evolve into something more. This song embodies self-preservation and detachment.

So, what does this song have to do with me? I'm glad you asked. This song is what set me on my path to writing this book. But first, I wrote a diss song. The diss track that should have won a Grammy:

<u>**Diss Track ; Dead To Me**</u>

"It wasn't all my fault because you were lying to me. Top down in the car, you were crying to me.

So depressed, how could you do this to me?

Now you're dead to me all the things you said to me.

I regret you, wish I could take back the day I met you.

If you were on fire man, you would get peed on.

I hope ya next chick leaves you for a bum,

Or you dumb, stupid, or dumb?

I'm really not the one, baby boy, you can have your fun.

I am not trying to be your girl.

Baby, you a bitch."

Blah! Blah! Blah!...

Yeah! As you can clearly tell, I was butt-hurt, and deep in my feelings. This relationship didn't cause any physical harm to any butts; However, he did make some strange requests. So let's talk about that. The Milking Situation, look it up...

This person who shall remain nameless was very interested in this.

Listen!

He wasn't exactly begging for anything. Let's just say it was a topic of multiple conversations. And I was curious but cautious.

As I'm writing this, I'm praying my mother never sees this story. This woman still doesn't know I have sex. My entire Jamaican family would disown me on sight if they knew what "milking was." Shit! Before this, I didn't know what it was.

So please, if you're reading this mind your business.

Dating Apps.

Let's talk about it & the delusion it provides on a platter. It all started on a dating app. Well...before that, it actually started on Clubhouse, where I was in a room talking absolute shit with my friends. The topic? Farting in front of a man you like.

Yes!

Farts!

Some men in the room said they would break up with a woman if she didn't get up and leave the room to fart. Others were way too into it.

Me? I don't care. Farts are natural.

The fuck!

If I need to fart, I'm gonna do what needs to be done. I then boldly declared.

"I want someone to love me for me farts and all."

Multiple men gasped, clutching their pearls.

Others? They said.

"Let me smell it."

One guy even had the audacity to say.

"Fart in my mouth."

And just like that, I realized… I might have accidentally attracted the wrong crowd. Still, I was intrigued. So, I went to my dating app bio and wrote:

"I fart on the first date."

And to this very day a week before my 35th birthday it's still there.

Surprisingly, not many men were turned off.

I got responses like:

"That's real. Let me smell it."

"Fart in my mouth, queen."

"Just know…I'm farting back."

I got what I asked for. But not quite what I was looking for. Enter's Grandpa App Bae.

Eventually, I stumbled across him. I'll keep names out of this, but his dating profile read something like this:

Homebody looking for love and someone to do a creative collaboration.

Bingo!

This is what I had been waiting for.

This man was screaming stability-ish or so I thought.

His profile told me he was ready to settle down and bonus points he was a photographer.

In my mind, I was manifesting the perfect match.

But what I didn't realize at the time was my own toxic trait; I was too open to shit I had no business being open to. Minor plot twist; From independent woman to almost-submissive. Imagine being hell-bent on never submitting to a man, only to start entertaining full-blown conversations about being a submissive in a Dom/Sub dynamic.

What the fuck!

Me, talking about letting a man control me.

Not just talking about it planning to act on it.

I told myself, "This is different. Maybe different is good?"

Insert side-eye's here.

How does this relate to the song? Well, let me tell you. Grandpa App Bae was making big plans before we even met. He was talking about flying me out to see some land he was buying on the West Coast. At first, I was unimpressed.

Bro, I work for an airline I can fly wherever I want, whenever I want for free. But this man wasn't trying to fly me out for sexual relations. He was genuinely trying to show me his vision board and bring me into it.

Or so I thought. But then... he got the call.

He got the job offer of his dreams... And just like that, he went from "Let's build something" to emotionally unavailable overnight. When we first started talking, he was asking me to make him a pumpkin pie.

I told him I would make it for his birthday, and if I don't make it, I'll buy it. His birthday came, and I offered to buy him one. Suddenly, he didn't want it. That pie became my breaking point after experiencing multiple cracks; Of course... Why would you turn down a pie you said you loved? The one you asked for.

Dummy!

That's when it hit me he was never planning to stay. And just like that... I realized I was holding on to something I had no business with.

I lost myself trying to hold on to someone who was already gone.

To Be Continued...

Because yes, I still talk to this man.But we're just friends.

Kind of.

Maybe.

I don't know.

We'll see.

Side Note

I wrote this in June 2024; It's April 2025. I haven't spoken to this man. And I don't want to. Not out of bitterness, but simply because I have no business talking to this man. I know how to mind my business in this relation-shit game.

Interlude
Open Verse

Poems & Shit

Tracy-Ann D. Thorpe

I Can't Keep My Eyes Off You

I can't keep my eyes off you.
I just can't keep my eyes off you.
You got a body like a god,
and I just want to climb you.
You know I want to ride you.
I just can't keep my eyes off you.
You got a smile like a
sunset ooh, it's getting me wet.
I just can't keep my eyes off you.
I just can't keep my eyes off you.

Heart Encounter

A night of void, lonely is the heart.
Where two souls meet, only a note apart.
Led by fate, lights in the
dark five floors in between, one beat of the heart.
A chance not taken is a chance not to start.
Follow your footsteps,
all the way to the heart.

Dope Shit

Having nice things is some dope shit.
But what does it matter if you don't have anyone to share it
with?
Imagine having everything you ever wanted in life and still
being unhappy.
Having all your needs met and still feeling empty.
Not to mention, no one calls you when you're alone.
So you're stuck looking at a dry phone, with no missed calls.
Imagine taking a ride on a rollercoaster,
then getting off and having no one to catch you when you
stumble.
When you're emotionally unstable and you're not able to
function like a normal person,
to not have someone to hold you when you crumble.
I don't want that, I want some dope shit.
I don't want to struggle,
I want someone I can build with,
so 10 years later we could look back and say,
damn, look at the life we built from the ground up.
Going from renting fast cars, driving around with the top
down blasting music.
To having a 6-car garage filled with nice cars.
From having debt to building wealth.
From broken homes to homes filled with
laughter to not knowing the end to a happily ever after.
I am chasing an endgame, not that I want my life to be over.

I just want it to start with someone I can share the same heart
with.
I say all that to say this:
I am just looking for some dope shit!

Forever

There was a time when I knew what I
knew no hesitation when it came to you.
You showed me love, that much was true.
My world would stop when it came to you.
For better or worse, love or pain.
If I lost you, I would go insane.
I'm forever yours.

A Peace You Found

Where do I start remembering,
collecting the pieces of my broken heart?
Crying in the dark or only shedding a tear when it rained,
because it's normal to have splashes of water on your face.
Why did no one notice?
Because I looked calm on the surface.
Always smiling, steady, happy, but slowly dying.
Is this love? Is this the miracle that everyone speaks of?
Does the hurt come with the territory?
I noticed my heart on my sleeve.
so I rolled my shirt down, never letting it see the sunshine in
the summer.
Now that I am healing, minding my business,
you came to me with one of the pieces you found
and asked if it was mine.
I said it looked familiar, but you were wasting your time.
That love shit don't live here anymore.
But you was
consistent showing me that you was not a waste of time.
Giving me the opportunity to really get to know you
and for you to know me.
Thank you for helping me to find my peace.

If Ever

If ever I get a chance to love again,
I would throw caution to the
wind crash into my lover's arms like waves on sand.
This would mean I would have to trust again.
Trust someone to care.
It would mean I felt safe.
Safe enough to tear down my walls.
It would mean sharing my time with
someone time I would never get back.
Is it worth it going through the cycle of love,
not knowing if I would end up with a happy ending or a
broken heart,
smiles or painful scars?
Knowing there is a person somewhere out there for me,
I'll set aside the time.
Brick by brick, I'll take down the wall.
Cuddled in his arms, I would feel safe.
I would do it.
If ever I had a chance to love again.

Love Siren

Put your number in my phone,

and I can take the pain away.

You can call on me.

You can call on me.

Put your number in my phone,

and I can take the pain away.

You can call on me.

You can call on me.

As our souls unwind,

we're magically inclined to decline the greatest love of all time.

Now you're sitting', stressing',

chasing' on depression,

only focused on the L's,

never focused on the lessons, right?

Put your number in my phone.

I just need someone to talk to

when I'm feeling lonely, damn!

It's crazy how your love was never mine.

Heart chakra stuck on stupid.

Throat chakra on decline.

And I...I

hope that you can hear me right now.

And I...I hope I'm speaking clearly right now.

Because you got me fucked up.

The way you got me fucked up.

Now I'm sitting' here crying',

looking' stupid.

What's sup?

Heavy

Heavy is the crown that's on my head.
Messages that go unread instead of reading.
You don't know the way I'm feeling.
You don't know.
But heavy is the crown that's on my soul.
I'm busy being lonely
when I'm scared of being lonely.
This is crazy feeling lonely.
That's the feeling when you're gone.
But heavy is the crown that's on my head.
The messages that go unread instead of reading.
You don't know the way I'm feeling.
You don't know.
But heavy is the crown that's on my soul.

Cold Heart

The way I'm feeling got me feeling
like I'm on cloud nine, touching on the ceiling.
I look at him, he look at
me deep down I get the feeling it could never be us.
Plain as day in the night sky,
I could see the moon looking in your eye.
I just knew that it could never be.
The way you look at her,
you never look at me.
And I never want to resent you.
I just knew that heaven sent you.
I just knew that it was never me.
The way I look at him you could never see.
I got one question that I gotta ask:
How can you see a future
looking at your past?
How can you see a future
looking at your past?
Cold heart, I love you.
I just can't help myself.
Still I want the love from someone else.
Don't know why I do this shit to myself.
Cold heart, I love you.
I can't help myself.

365

I know that you don't love me
the way that you once loved
me like right before you started hating me
for all the things that I've done.
I'm writing you this apology.
So, baby, please acknowledge me.
I just want to tell you
I'm sorry for all the things that I've done.
I'm needing you
like I need breath in my
life 24/7 and 365.
I don't want to lie,
and I don't want to cry.
I don't don't want to be alone.
I don't want to be alone.

Outro
A Tribute

This book is a tribute to GIVĒON, my spirit guide through heartbreaks. His music helped me name the feelings I never had words for. A song inspired each chapter in this story. Songs that brought clarity, inspiration, or healing to a feeling I once; experienced, witnessed, heard about, or even dished out. This work is not affiliated or endorsed by GIVĒON or his label. It is a fan-made homage rooted in deep gratitude and adoration.

Thank you for giving us the soundtrack to healing.

- Tracy- Ann

Connect With Me

Want more?
Follow, subscribe, or vibe with me below.
Email: info@goodjinx.com
To submit your own love stories or find upcoming books and
issues, visit.
Website: www.goodjinx.com

Note from the Author

I did everything in this book myself the formatting, the editing, the cover, all of it with zero dollars and a broken heart.
If you catch a typo or something off, feel free to send me a message. I'll fix it in the second edition.
This isn't a perfect book.
It's a real one.
And I hope it found you when you needed it most.

www.ingramcontent.com/pod-product-compliance
Lightning Source LLC
Chambersburg PA
CBHW011519100726
47899CB00010BD/3432